Dear Parent:
Your child's love of reading starts here!

Every child learns to read in a different way and at his or her own speed. Some go back and forth between reading levels and read favorite books again and again. Others read through each level in order. You can help your young reader improve and become more confident by encouraging his or her own interests and abilities. From books your child reads with you to the first books he or she reads alone, there are I Can Read Books for every stage of reading:

SHARED READING
Basic language, word repetition, and whimsical illustrations, ideal for sharing with your emergent reader

BEGINNING READING
Short sentences, familiar words, and simple concepts for children eager to read on their own

READING WITH HELP
Engaging stories, longer sentences, and language play for developing readers

READING ALONE
Complex plots, challenging vocabulary, and high-interest topics for the independent reader

ADVANCED READING
Short paragraphs, chapters, and exciting themes for the perfect bridge to chapter books

I Can Read Books have introduced children to the joy of reading since 1957. Featuring award-winning authors and illustrators and a fabulous cast of beloved characters, I Can Read Books set the standard for beginning readers.

A lifetime of discovery begins with the magical words "I Can Read!"

Visit www.icanread.com for information on enriching your child's reading experience.

HARRY
and the
Lady Next Door

HARRY and

Pictures by
Margaret Bloy Graham

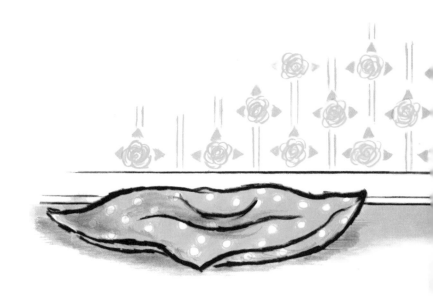

the Lady Next Door

WITHDRAWN

by Gene Zion

HarperCollins*Publishers*

Library of Congress Catalog Card Number: 60-9452
ISBN-10: 0-06-026852-2 (lib. bdg.) — ISBN-13: 978-0-06-026852-7 (lib. bdg.)
ISBN-10: 0-06-444008-7 (pbk.) — ISBN-13: 978-0-06-444008-0 (pbk.)
❖
16 17 18 PC/WOR 16 15 14 13 12

CONTENTS

THE PARTY

Harry was a white dog
with black spots.
He loved all his neighbors,
all except one.
He did not love the lady next door.

The lady next door sang.

She sang high and loud.

When she sang, Harry's ears hurt.

She sang higher

than the peanut whistle.

When she sang, the peanut man

put his hands over his ears.

She sang louder
than the siren on the fire engine.
When she sang, the firemen
put their hands over their ears.

She sang higher and louder

than the cats sang.

When she sang, the cats ran away.

Harry tried everything to make her stop.

He howled under her window.

His friends howled too.

But it did not do any good.

The lady next door went on singing.

She sang higher and louder than ever.

One day Harry's family gave a party.

They invited the lady next door.

She came with her music.

When she started to sing,

Harry almost bit her leg.

But he bit the leg of the piano instead.

The family sent Harry

out of the room.

"You are a bad dog,"

they said.

Harry just wagged his tail.

As he walked to the door
some people said,
"Poor Harry."
But others whispered,
"The lucky dog!"

When Harry pushed the door open

the wind blew in.

It blew the pages of music off the piano.

They blew all around the room.

Everyone tried to catch the music

but no one could.

The pages blew out the door

and into the garden.

They blew over the fence

and up into the trees.

Harry caught some of the pages

but he did not bring them back.

He ran away with them.

HARRY'S FIRST TRY

He ran until he came to a quiet spot.

He dropped the music and lay down.

Soon he fell asleep.

In a little while,
something woke Harry up.

All around him were cows mooing.

They mooed very low notes.

Harry listened.

He thought the cows

made beautiful music.

He had never heard anything
so soft and low.
He wished the lady next door
would sing like the cows.
Suddenly Harry had an idea.

He rounded up all the cows.

He barked at their heels.

Down the road they went.

Harry barked and the cows mooed.

They ran on and on.

They ran down the main street of town.

They passed the school, the library

and the fire house.

When they came to Harry's house
the lady was still singing.
Harry ran ahead and stopped the cows.
They went on mooing.
They mooed and mooed and mooed.

They all mooed soft and low.

The cows mooed for a long time

but it did not do any good.

The lady next door went on singing.

She sang higher and louder than ever.

Harry's family called the man

who owned the cows.

He came and took them home.

That night,

Harry slept in the dog house.

HARRY'S SECOND TRY

The next day

the lady next door sang some more.

Harry's ears hurt more than ever.

He went for a walk.

After he had walked for a long time

he heard a wonderful sound.

"Oompah! Oompah! Oompah! Oompah!"

It was low and lovely.

Then Harry saw what it was.

It was the big horn
in the Firemen's Band.

The big horn was even softer and lower
than cows mooing.

Harry walked along listening.

He wished the lady next door

would sing like the big horn.

Then he saw the leader of the band.

The leader threw his stick into the air.

Harry watched.

Suddenly he had an idea.

The next time

the stick went into the air,

Harry caught it.

Harry ran in front of the band.

The leader ran after Harry—

and the band ran after the leader.

Soon the leader was all out of breath.

He stopped running.

But the band ran after Harry.

The men played as they ran.

Harry led them all

down the main street of town.

They passed the school, the library

and the fire house.

Harry stopped the band
in front of the lady's house.
She was still singing.
The big horn player played
even softer and lower than before.

He blew and blew and blew

right under her window.

But it did not do any good.

The lady next door went on singing.

She sang higher and louder than ever.

When the leader got there
he had Harry's family with him.
Harry gave the stick back.

That night,

he slept in the dog house again.

THE CONTEST

A few nights after that,

the family took Harry to the park.

They were going to hear

the Firemen's Band.

The family knew that Harry liked

the big horn.

They got to the park and sat down.

A light shone on the stage.

The people were quiet.

They waited for the music to begin.

Harry closed his eyes and listened.

He waited for the big horn.

He waited for the soft, low notes.

But the low notes never came.

Instead, a man came out.

"Good evening, friends," he said.

"The band will not play tonight.

The big horn player is all out of breath.

Instead, we shall have a singing contest.

And here are the ladies who will sing."

Everyone clapped

when the ladies came out.

On the end of the line

was the lady next door.

Harry took one look

and ran off.

He was almost out of the park

when he heard something.

"Blurp Blurp."

"Blurp Blurp."

It was low and beautiful.

Harry stopped and listened.

It was even softer and lower

than the cows and the big horn.

He wished the lady next door

would sing like this.

Then he saw where the sound came from.

It came from inside a watering can.

Suddenly Harry had an idea.

He took the handle of the can

in his mouth.

Then he ran with it.

When he got back to the bandstand,
he walked quietly up the stairs.
The lady next door was singing.

Harry put the watering can
on the floor behind her.

51

Soon the lady sang a *very* high note.

Then something happened.

Two frogs jumped out of the can.

One jumped on the lady's head.

The other jumped on her shoulder.

The other ladies in the contest

shrieked and ran from the stage.

But the lady next door went on singing.

She sang higher and louder than ever.

When she finished her song,

everyone shouted, "Hooray!"

The judges whispered together.

Then one of them spoke.

"Ladies and gentlemen," he said.

"The other ladies in the contest

have all gone home.

So the lady next door wins

the singing contest!

She is a *brave* lady.

She wins First Prize.

It means she can study music

in a far-off country

for a long time!"

Everyone clapped and clapped.

Harry barked and barked.

He was the happiest of all.

In the middle of all the fuss

the frogs hopped home.

Soon the time came

for the lady next door

to go away.

Harry went to the ship

with the family

to see her off.

"Good-bye! Good-bye!" everyone shouted

Harry wagged his tail.

The lady next door started to sing

a good-bye song.

But no one ever heard her.

Just as she sang the first note

the ship blew its foghorn.

It was a deep, low, wonderful sound. As the ship moved away from the dock, other boats blew their foghorns too.

Harry thought it was
the most beautiful good-bye song
he had ever heard.

The End